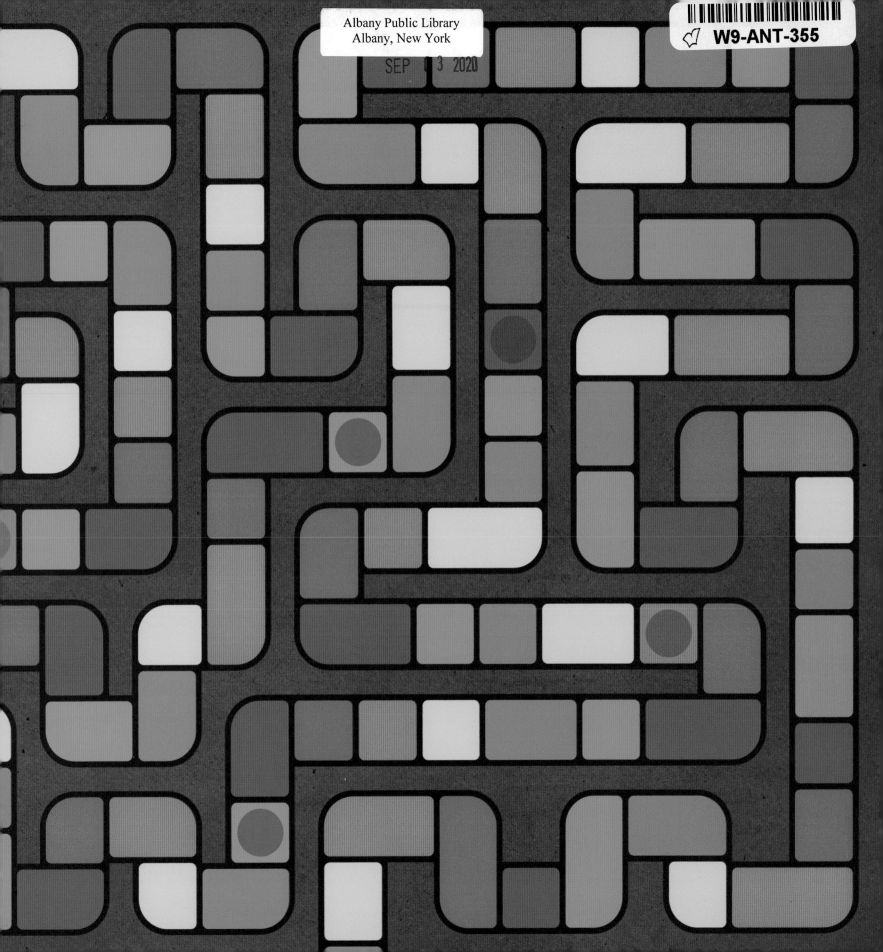

DO NOT EAT the GAME!

Matthew McElligott

CROWN BOOKS
FOR YOUNG READERS
New York

For Christy and for Anthony,
a winner who never gives up

Text copyright © 2020 by Matthew McElligott

Jacket art and interior illustrations copyright © 2020 by Matthew McElligott

Visit us on the Web! rhcbooks.com

Educators and librarians, for a variety of teaching tools, visit us at RHTeachersLibrarians.com

Library of Congress Cataloging-in-Publication Data
Names: McElligott, Matthew, author, illustrator.
Title: Do not eat the game! / Matthew McElligott.
Description: First edition. | New York : Crown Books for Young Readers, [2020] | Audience: Ages 5–8.
| Audience: Grades K–1. | Summary: "A girl tries to play a game with monsters, but it quickly turns
into chaos when they don't follow the rules"—Provided by publisher.
Identifiers: LCCN 2019032846 (print) | LCCN 2019032847 (ebook) | ISBN 978-1-5247-6723-5
(hardcover) | ISBN 978-1-5247-6724-2 (library binding) | ISBN 978-1-5247-6725-9 (ebook)
Subjects: CYAC: Games—Fiction. | Monsters—Fiction. | Humorous stories.
Classification: LCC PZ7.M478448 Do 2020 (print) | LCC PZ7.M478448 (ebook) | DDC [E]—dc23

The text of this book is set in 18-point New Century Schoolbook and 23-point Kidprint.
The illustrations in this book were created using a combination of pencil and digital techniques.

MANUFACTURED IN CHINA
10 9 8 7 6 5 4 3 2 1

First Edition

This game is for two
or more players.

And don't
worry . . .

Read all
the rules.

Carefully take
everything out of
the box.

Do not throw the pieces.

Do not eat the game.

Roll the dice. Take turns moving around the board.

Every time you land on a color,

find a block that matches and add it to your tower.

Build your tower carefully.

If your tower falls,

you're out of the game, and the next player
gets your blocks.

The more players
there are . . .

. . . the more
fun you'll have!

If you have to
pause the game,

be careful not to move
any of the pieces,

The game ends when one player has all the pieces.

When the game is over,

don't forget to put all the pieces away.

And always
remember
to have fun!

This game is for two
or more players.

Every time you land on
a square, do what it says.

EAT THE GAME!

THROW THE
PIECES!

STAND ON
YOUR HEAD!

This game is for two or more players.

The more players there are,
the more fun you'll have!

And it's a great way
to make new friends.

Do not eat the game.

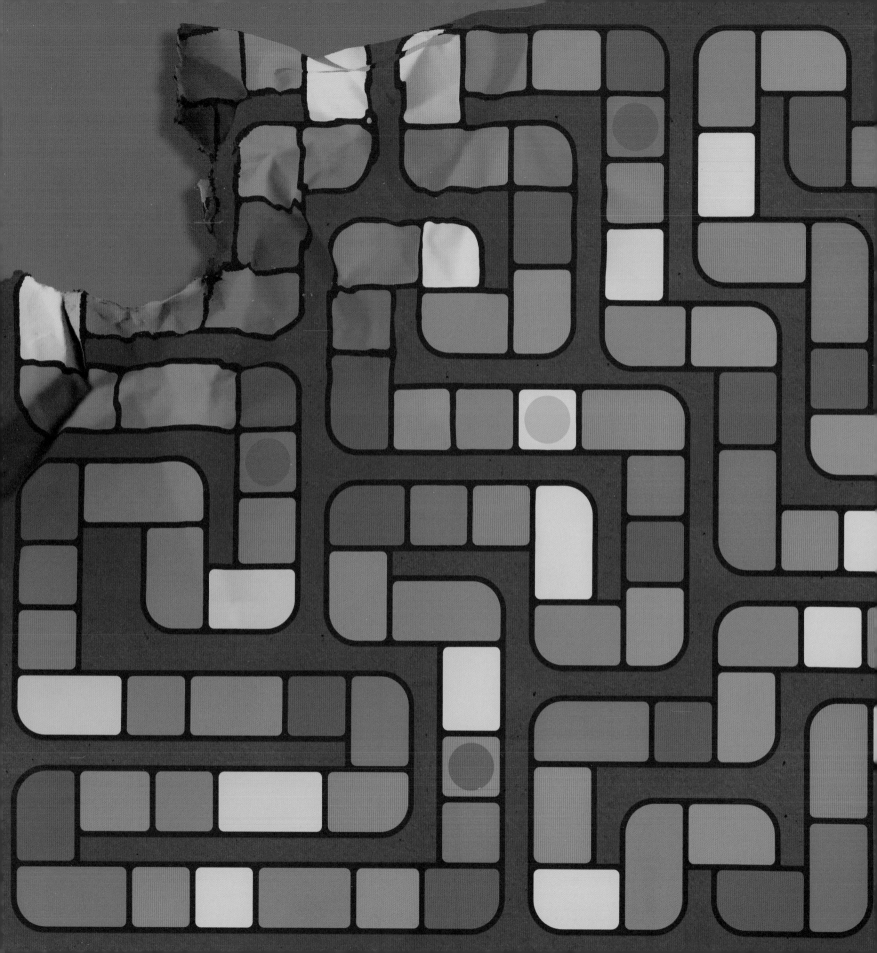